KT-363-618

Mortaxe

The Skeleton Warrior

BY ADAM BLADE

ORCHARD

Mortaxe
The Skeleton Warrior

Mortaxe the Skeleton Warrior was originally
published as Beast Quest and This

C333892251

*You will earn one special gold coin for every chapter
you finish. Find out what to do with your
coins at the back of the book!*

With special thanks to Michael Ford and
Fiona Munro

Reading Consultant: Prue Goodwin, lecturer in literacy and
children's books

ORCHARD BOOKS
Carmelite House
50 Victoria Embankment
London EC4Y 0DZ

Mortaxe the Skeleton Warrior first published in 2010
This Early Reader edition published in 2016
Text © Beast Quest Limited 2010, 2016
Cover and inside illustrations by Steve Sims © Beast Quest Limited 2010, 2016

A CIP catalogue record for this book is available from the British Library.

ISBN 978 1 40834 182 7

Printed in China

The paper and board used in this book are made from wood
from responsible sources.

Orchard Books
An imprint of Hachette Children's Group
Part of The Watts Publishing Group Limited
An Hachette UK Company

www.hachette.co.uk
www.beastquest.co.uk

Beasts of Avantia
THE PIT OF FIRE
MALVEL'S MAZE
STONEWIN VOLCANO
ERRINEL
THE DEAD VALLEY
THE DEAD JUNGLE
THE DARK WOOD
THE DARK JUNGLE

TOM

Heroic fighter of
Beasts and saviour
of Avantia

ELENNA

Tom's trusted
friend and loyal
companion

ADURO

The Good Wizard
who serves King Hugo
and guides Tom

STORM

Tom's brave
stallion

SILVER

Elenna's pet
wolf

MALVEL

The Evil Wizard.
He is Tom's main
enemy

KING
HUGO

King of
Avantia

PETRA

One of
Malvel's evil
helpers

MORTAXE

A skeleton monster with the
heart of a cursed bull Beast

CONTENTS

STORY ONE

The Calm Before the Storm

It has been an honour for Silver and me to join Tom on his Quests – together we have never failed.

But our enemies do not rest. Keep reading, if you think your heart is as strong as mine.

Chapter 1

An Explosion

Tom sighed as he pulled on his robe and looked down at his feet in their sparkling slippers. He didn't feel very comfortable, but it was King Hugo's birthday, and he was a guest at the castle. The clothes had been left in his bedchamber, and a servant had asked him to try the outfit on.

Suddenly, Tom's door flew open. It was Elenna.

"Just look what they've done to me!" she said angrily.

His good friend wore a shimmering yellow dress and had a tiara plonked on the top of her short, spiky hair. Tom tried hard not to giggle.

Suddenly, there was a loud bang outside and Tom rushed to the window. As Tom looked around, there came another loud noise, but this time an orange light burst above the turrets like a firework.

"Look!" said Elenna, pointing.

Aduro was standing on a patch of bare ground.

"He must be preparing fireworks for the celebrations!" Tom laughed.

Whistling loudly, Tom managed to get the Good Wizard's attention, just as yet another explosion rattled the windows and shook the walls.

Tom frowned. This was not a firework display. This was something else. Something bad.

As smoke rose into the sky, Aduro began to run.

"Go and change," said Tom, tearing off the grand robes and grabbing his shield and sword. "I'll meet you downstairs."

A few minutes later, Tom and Elenna hurried towards the site of the explosion.

The smoke had almost cleared when they caught up with the Good Wizard in a far corner of the dark stables. They watched as he threw hay bales aside, revealing a trapdoor.

Aduro tapped the door with his staff. It creaked open to reveal stone steps.

"These lead to the Gallery of Tombs," he explained. "The explosion was down there."

Tom looked at Elenna in surprise. He had no idea this place existed.

Aduro led the way down the stairs into the dark until, at last, they reached the bottom. Walking one behind the other, they followed a narrow passage. Thick cobwebs hung from the mossy walls.

As the tunnel widened, Tom could see stone caskets standing up against the walls.

"This place must be hundreds of years old," Elenna muttered.

"The Gallery of Tombs is older than the castle itself," said Aduro quietly. "Every Master of Beasts is buried here. If the Gallery has been disturbed then evil must be close by."

Chapter 2

Petra

Exploring further, they came across two caskets laid in front of them. Tom read the letters on the first. 'TANNER, FIRST MASTER OF THE BEASTS'

The tomb beside Tanner's read simply 'MORTAXE'.

Before Tom could ask Aduro about the tombs, a beam of light exploded from the shadows, knocking him backwards.

Another beam hit Aduro,
pinning him to the ground.

"Come closer and I'll snap
his bones like twigs," came
a girl's sneering voice. In the
semi-darkness Tom made
out the figure of a girl with
glowing eyes.

"You don't look much like a hero," said the ghostly figure to Tom. "But then Malvel always did call you an annoying little runt."

Malvel. Tom should have known he would be behind this.

"I am Petra," the girl continued. "And together, Malvel and I are going to take over the whole of Avantia."

Tom felt his anger burn as he charged at her.

A look of fury crossed Petra's face as she lifted her arm to fire another bolt of light at him. Tom brought up his sword as the fierce power brought rocks tumbling down around him.

"Did you really think it would be that easy?" Petra said as she sprang off the ground and hovered high up in the chamber, looking down at Tom.

"Come down here and fight!" Tom demanded.

Petra sneered as a beam fired from her finger into the tomb of Mortaxe. As Tom watched in horror, something like molten metal spread over the tomb's surface. The stone caved in, revealing a black space within.

"Arise, Mortaxe," Petra said in a whisper.

Tom watched in horror as five fingers crept over the edge of the tomb. He took a step back.

Something evil had arrived.

Chapter 3

Mortaxe

Mortaxe was like no Beast Tom had ever seen before. He looked like a human skeleton, but was more than twice the height of the tallest person Tom had ever met. The terrifying creature faced Tom, glaring at him with empty eyes that glowed red.

Mortaxe climbed out of the tomb. Tom stared at the Beast's chest, where a heart the size of a

human head was beating. Tom
looked over in panic at Aduro,
still trapped by Petra.

"Welcome back, Mortaxe!"
Petra called out. "Your time has
come again!"

The Beast grabbed a weapon from his tomb. Tom leapt forwards and blocked the blow as it came. Mortaxe roared, hurling Tom aside. Elenna shot an arrow towards Petra. The evil girl lost concentration and the beam of energy keeping Aduro

captive fell. The wizard was free. He stood up dizzily and spread his arms. In each hand a ball of light appeared. He sent them spinning towards Petra. There was a crash as she shot her own light back.

"You will not defeat us," Petra said fiercely.

Petra soared down to the
chamber floor and scurried into
the shadows. Tom and Elenna

charged at Mortaxe. The Beast bellowed with rage as he slashed with his weapon. As Tom ducked, he felt the blade slice through his hair. He leapt forwards and stabbed at the Beast's heart, but Mortaxe turned and Tom's blade was caught between his ribs.

"Stand back!" called Aduro suddenly. As Tom leapt away, the wizard hurled a spinning orb of light towards Mortaxe. But the Beast swept the ball aside, and rushed away with his evil partner, Petra.

Catching his breath, Aduro began to explain. "Mortaxe was once a brave soldier called Tarik. He fought alongside Tanner, but fell victim to the spell of a Dark Wizard. Tarik's good heart was still strong so the wizard swapped it for the heart of a cursed bull Beast. Now Mortaxe has the power to turn all Beasts to his evil will."

Aduro urged Tom to prise an etched map from the top of Tanner's tomb. As Tom held it up, his shield began to vibrate

and his brain was filled with
the bellows of distressed Beasts.

"Something terrible is
happening," he said.

1

Chapter 4

Good Beasts Turned Evil

Tom heard Aduro's voice close to his ear. "Mortaxe's will has touched the Beasts already."

"We must go," said Tom, as he and Elenna raced back along the passage and out into the stables. They both jumped onto Storm's back as Elenna whistled for Silver.

Tom checked the map and saw a tiny Mortaxe moving towards the Central Plains.

Shriek!

Soaring through the air above them was Epos, the Flame Bird. She turned into a steep dive and Tom was shocked to see the fireball between her claws.

"Look out," he said. "She's going to attack!"

Epos hurled the fireball towards them. Tom just managed to steer Storm away from its burning path.

"Epos is a Good Beast," cried Tom. "But Mortaxe has already used his wicked powers to make her evil."

They rode on, leaving the great creature circling above. At last they came to the Central Plains, where Mortaxe should have been, but all was empty and silent.

"Where is he?" asked Elenna,

looking across the endless land.

Before Tom could answer, they heard a deep groan come from a patch of ground ahead. A crack opened up and from it rose a wall of stone.

The wall grew into a vast circle all around them. Six arches appeared in the sides, with long benches made of stone.

"It's an arena!" whispered Elenna.

The ground shook further as a huge carved chair emerged. Mortaxe was sitting in it, gripping his weapon and now wearing

chest armour. Petra was standing
close by.

"Look!" said Tom, pointing at
the six arches. Elenna gasped as
she made out the six Good Beasts
of Avantia. Normally the sight of
the Beasts filled Tom with wonder.
Now there was only anger. How
dare anyone poison their noble
hearts with evil magic?

STORY TWO

Battle of the Beasts

Tom and I are marching right into the heart of the battle between Avantia's Good Beasts.

But how can my friend possibly survive a battle against a Skeleton Warrior who has such immense power over the Good Beasts?

Chapter 1
Arena of Death

The Beasts roared together, blasting anger and hatred.

"This place is for combat," said Tom. "The Beasts are going to be made to fight each other."

Running towards them, Tom saw that he was right. Ferno and Nanook faced each other.

Ferno reared back and fire shot from his mouth. The Snow Monster bellowed and Tom could smell burning fur.

Nanook stamped towards
Ferno, gripping one wing to
pull the dragon off balance.

"Don't hurt each other!"
Tom called desperately.

Suddenly Ferno swept down,
as Sepron wrapped his long
neck around Nanook's leg.

As Tom tried to help Nanook, Tagus the Horse-Man charged, battering them with his hooves. Moments later, Arcta the Mountain Giant was set upon by Ferno and knocked to the ground.

Tom looked round for Elenna. He desperately needed her help. But as he locked eyes with her, he heard her speak to Ferno. The words chilled his very bones.

"That's right!" said his once loyal friend. "Kill him!"

"You have to help me!" he said.

Elenna grinned. "From now on, I only help myself," she said coldly.

Tom couldn't believe what he was hearing. Could Mortaxe's magic really be so strong?

Mortaxe was laughing, but there was worse. Silver and Storm were at the foot of the Skeleton Warrior's throne. Suddenly, Storm kicked Silver hard, sending him flying across the arena. Tom gasped. They too had been bewitched.

Tom's gaze returned to the fight. Ferno had broken away from Arcta and had now been joined in the sky by Epos the Flame Bird. The two Beasts dived at one another, blasting jets of fire. They clashed and fell in a tangled heap of burning feathers.

Tom looked around with anger. Six Good Beasts were suffering. It was time to end this.

He held his sword high.

"You won't get away with this!" Tom shouted to Petra. "While there's blood in my veins. . ."

"Don't you ever get bored of saying that?" Elenna laughed cruelly.

Tom turned as he heard a great thudding noise coming closer. It was Mortaxe.

"This arena was built for death, and death there will be," Petra spat.

Mortaxe stood in the centre

of the arena. He towered over
Tom. His eyes showed no pity.
Tom had no doubt this would
be a duel to the death, and he
knew he was completely on
his own.

1

Chapter 2

The Battle Continues

As Tom gripped his shield, he saw the Beasts return to their arches. Several were bleeding and in pain.

As the sky darkened and lightning flashed across the sky, the evil Mortaxe turned his skull upwards. Tom saw his chance. He rushed forward and struck at the Beast with his sword.

The evil Beast yelled and slashed with his weapon,

knocking Tom off his feet. As
Tom struggled to get up, he came
face to face with Storm. The
stallion rushed at Tom, thrusting
with his head. Tom cried out as
he was pushed backwards.

Mortaxe peered down at Tom, as the Beasts of Avantia roared and screeched in excitement.

The Skeleton Warrior's weapon crashed down again. Tom managed to roll aside and scramble up.

Tom drove his sword into Mortaxe's knee. It seemed to be made of stone. How could Tom fight a Beast that was already dead?

Tom suddenly knew what he had to do. Mortaxe may have

been a skeleton, but his heart
was still alive. His heart was the
part given to the Beast by the
Dark Wizard. This was the key
to Mortaxe's power, but Tom
couldn't do it alone.

Elenna was watching with
an arrow in her bow. Tom
could see it tracking him as he
moved around.

Mortaxe raised his weapon and lunged, just as Tom tried to drive his sword through the thick leather of the Beast's breastplate. Tom was aiming for the heart. Mortaxe was enraged and came at Tom again.

Tom felt real fear. Even if he managed to get to the heart and defeat the Beast, Petra was waiting with her magic and Elenna was ready with an arrow. Then there would still be Storm, Silver and six angry Beasts to face.

Tom knew Elenna was still watching him. She wouldn't hesitate to fire her arrow.

Maybe there is a way to get Elenna's help, even if she doesn't want to give it, he thought.

Tom pretended to fall and Mortaxe did as he had hoped. The Beast reached out with a bony hand and gripped Tom by the throat, holding him up in the air for all to see.

"You always got in the way," Tom croaked to Elenna. "The Quests would have been

much easier if you'd just stayed
at home."

Elenna's face went white
with rage. She fired her arrow
directly at him.

1

Chapter 3

Mortaxe's Power

Tom jerked his body upwards, breaking Mortaxe's grip and feeling the arrow swish past him. As Tom fell to the ground, he looked up and saw the arrow buried deep in the Beast's eye socket.

"Got you!" he shouted.

The Skeleton Warrior roared and staggered. He swung his weapon and Tom watched as

the Beast sliced through his own chest armour, revealing his heart.

Before Tom had a chance to work out what to do next, the Beast used his free hand to tug the arrow from his eye and snap it.

As Tom staggered against a wall, the furious Beast took mighty steps towards him. Tom managed to turn aside at the last minute and Mortaxe brought his weapon down into solid stone. At once, Tom gripped his sword and turned to the distracted Beast.

"My turn!" he shouted.

Tom brought down the blade on Mortaxe's arm. He sliced it clean off.

Mortaxe gave a roar of anger. Tom reached for the

wooden handle of the Beast's weapon and with a grunt of effort pulled it free from the stone.

"Enough!" screamed Petra. "Kill him, Mortaxe!"

Tom glanced up and could see Malvel's evil apprentice high above. A wicked light shone in Petra's eyes as she rubbed her hands.

"I don't think so," Tom muttered under his breath.

It took all Tom's strength to lift the Beast's weapon. With a yell, he heaved it across Mortaxe's chest, finally exposing the Beast's heart.

Around the edges of the arena, the once Good and brave Beasts of Avantia roared and screeched in anger. Storm and Silver growled and kicked at the ground nearby. Everyone was against Tom.

Chapter 4
The Battle is Won

With his hands, Tom reached
into the Skeleton Warrior's chest
and grasped the Beast's evil
heart. Tom pulled it free.

The Beast's mouth opened.
No sound came out. Then,
incredibly, Mortaxe's bones
began to fall apart in front
of Tom. Any life there had
been within Mortaxe's deep eye
sockets was gone.

"No!" screamed Petra. "It can't be!"

Tom threw the heart aside. A huge shadow fell over him. The Beasts were approaching.

"I don't want to fight you,"
Tom said to them desperately.
The huge creatures formed

a semi-circle around Tom. He picked up his sword, but he knew he couldn't hold off six Beasts.

With a screech, Epos suddenly hurled a fireball, but not at Tom. It crashed into the arena wall, making the whole place shake and creating a great hole. Rocks tumbled to the ground. Tom waited for one of the creatures to attack. But it didn't happen. Instead, one by one, the Good Beasts moved away from him.

Tagus kicked away great chunks of stone. Arcta pushed against a wall until it crumbled and fell.

The Beasts were destroying the arena! Tom couldn't help the smile that spread across his face. Mortaxe's spell was broken!

"What are you doing?" Petra shouted to them.

The Beasts on the ground continued to heave the great stones away. Above, Ferno swooped towards the evil witch,

breathing fire. In a cloud of
smoke, Petra vanished.

As the smoke cleared, Tom
caught sight of Elenna lying on
the ground. Her skin was pale
and her eyes closed.

The air was thick with smoke and the whole ground seemed to shake like an earthquake. Tom carried his friend from the now burning and crumbling arena. They collapsed on the soft grass outside. Rolling over, Tom saw the Beasts escaping to safety after them.

Elenna's eyelids flickered, then opened.

"What happened? I don't remember anything," she said, putting out her hand to stroke

her faithful wolf, Silver, now gentle and calm once more.

"Tom, did we argue?" she asked, confused. "I seem to remember we did."

"I don't know what you're talking about," he said smiling. "When do we ever argue?"

If you enjoyed this story, you may want to read

Creta
The Winged Terror

EARLY READER

Here's how the story begins...

Tom felt happy as he stared up at a sky full of stars. He was camping in the mountains with his father, Taladon, who was Avantia's Master of Beasts.

It was a humid night and as Tom wiped his forehead he felt something crawling on his skin. Brushing it off, he could see it was some kind of cockroach, its black shell gleaming in the moonlight. "Urgh!" he exclaimed, watching it fly away. Then Tom let out a gasp – the ground was crawling with insects, some creeping on the sleeping Taladon. Tom jumped to his feet, waking his father.

"What are they?" Tom asked

as the stinking black-shelled creatures scuttled around his feet.

"I don't know," his father replied, puzzled, as the swarm skimmed close to their heads and were gone.

Something about the insects unsettled Tom, but after a few moments he and his father settled back down beside the fire. The smoke seemed to be moving...taking shape...

Tom's eyes widened. There was the face of his friend

Elenna, who, together with her wolf, Silver, had accompanied him on his Quests. She looked worried.

"Avantia is suffering from an infestation of some kind of bug," she said. "The kingdom needs your help!"

READ

Creta

The Winged Terror

EARLY READER

TO FIND OUT WHAT HAPPENS NEXT!

LEARN TO READ WITH

EARLY READER

Beast Quest®

Beast Quest Early Readers are easy-to-read versions of the bestselling Beast Quest books, specially adapted for developing readers

Perfect for parents to read aloud and for newly confident readers to read along

Remember to enjoy reading together. It's never too early to share a story!

CONGRATULATIONS,
YOU HAVE COMPLETED THIS QUEST!

At the end of each chapter you were awarded a special gold coin. The QUEST in this book was worth an amazing **8** coins.

Look at the Beast Quest totem picture inside the back cover of this book to see how far you've come in your journey to become

MASTER OF THE BEASTS.

The more books you read, the more coins you will collect!

Do you want your own Beast Quest Totem?

1. Copy the coin below
2. Go to the Beast Quest website
3. Download and print out your totem
4. Add your coin to the totem

www.beastquest.co.uk/totem

Beast Quest®

TOP TRUMPS
COLLECTOR CARDS INSIDE!
FREE

Series 1
COLLECT THEM ALL!

Meet Tom, Elenna and the first six Beasts!

FERNO
THE FIRE DRAGON
978-1-84616-483-5

SEPRON
THE SEA SERPENT
978-1-84616-482-8

ARCTA
THE MOUNTAIN GIANT
978-1-84616-484-2

TAGUS
THE HORSE-MAN
978-1-84616-486-6

NANOOK
THE SNOW MONSTER
978-1-84616-485-9

EPOS
THE FLAME BIRD
978-1-84616-487-3